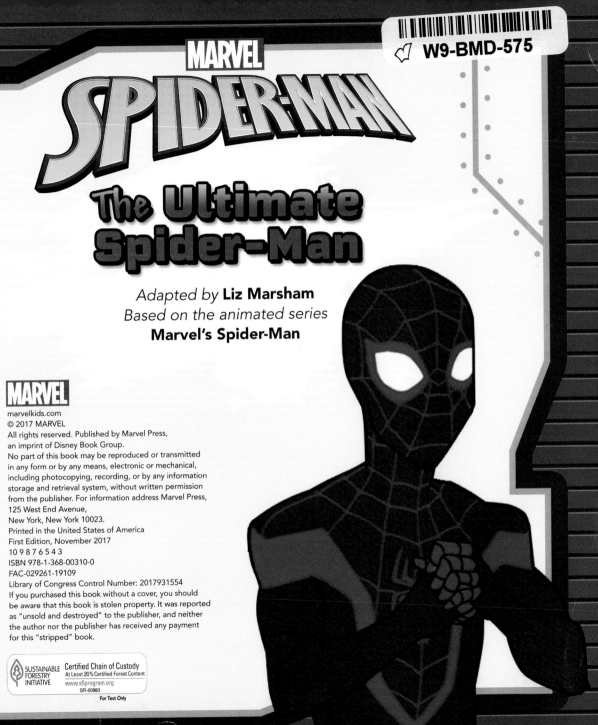

MARVEL

SPIDER-MAN

The Ultimate Spider-Man

Adapted by **Liz Marsham**
Based on the animated series
Marvel's Spider-Man

MARVEL

marvelkids.com
© 2017 MARVEL
All rights reserved. Published by Marvel Press,
an imprint of Disney Book Group.
No part of this book may be reproduced or transmitted
in any form or by any means, electronic or mechanical,
including photocopying, recording, or by any information
storage and retrieval system, without written permission
from the publisher. For information address Marvel Press,
125 West End Avenue,
New York, New York 10023.
Printed in the United States of America
First Edition, November 2017
10 9 8 7 6 5 4 3
ISBN 978-1-368-00310-0
FAC-029261-19109
Library of Congress Control Number: 2017931554

SUSTAINABLE
FORESTRY
INITIATIVE

Certified Chain of Custody
At Least 20% Certified Forest Content
www.sfiprogram.org
SFI-00993

For Text Only

The strangest day of Miles Morales's life started with the bullies. They grabbed him outside his apartment. But they ran when they saw Miles's father.

"I can take care of myself, Dad," Miles said.

Miles's friend Peter Parker walked up. He had seen the whole thing.

Peter said he used to get bullied, too. But the bullying didn't bother him, because he knew he was making good choices. "That's *real* power," he told Miles.

"That's not power!" Miles replied. "You watch, I just haven't had my growth spurt yet, but man, when I do people are gonna say—"

Peter interrupted, pointing toward the sky. **"Oh no!"**

Peter was pointing at a huge **purple robot** climbing the side of a tall building.

"There's some sort of slayer headed for Osborn Academy!" Peter said as he ran down the street.

"I'm coming, too!" Miles shouted after him.

At the top of the Osborn Academy building, the slayer faced Norman Osborn. A scientist named Spencer Smythe had stolen the robot from Osborn and was driving it by remote control. He would destroy the slayer unless Osborn surrendered his supersecret technology.

SMASH!

Spider-Man swung through the window and knocked the slayer over. He used his webs to swing the robot onto the roof, but time was running out.

BOOM!

The slayer exploded and knocked Spider-Man off the roof!

Miles raced toward the Osborn Academy gates. "Gotta get inside to help Peter," he panted. Then, **BAM!** Miles crashed right into Spencer Smythe! Smythe dropped his case on the ground, and a vial fell out.

"Sorry, let me help," Miles said, picking up the vial. Miles felt a sharp pain in his hand. Something had bit him!

Then Miles saw Spider-Man falling off the roof. There was no time to think. He had to help. Miles leaped way, way up into the air, and he caught Spider-Man in his arms just in time!

"How did I just do that?" he wondered. "Uh, I think I'm gonna be sick!" He ran off before Spider-Man could wake up.

In a secret underground room, Smythe met with his partner. They had used the slayer as a distraction while Smythe stole Osborn's super-spiders.

But when they opened the case, they saw that one of the vials was gone. They needed the DNA of that missing spider!

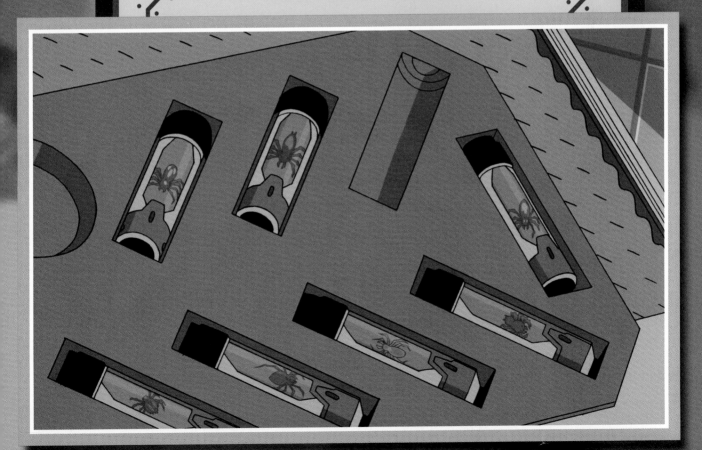

Norman Osborn realized that his spiders had been taken. They were dangerous in the wrong hands. So, Osborn had a plan if the spiders were ever stolen: an army of slayers!

Alistair Smythe, Spencer's son, worked for Osborn. Osborn told Alistair to get one of the slayers ready.

Meanwhile, Peter got a call from Miles. When he went to Miles's room, he found Miles dressed in a black-and-red Spider-Man suit! Miles had been bitten by a spider and had all of Spider-Man's powers. He couldn't wait to show them off to everyone.

Miles jumped from the ceiling. **"This is the greatest day of my life!"**

Miles rushed right out to tell his friends Anya and Gwen.
"Maybe we can all get spider-powers!" Anya said.
Peter couldn't believe what he was hearing. He kept his identity hidden for a reason. "Guys! You talk about these powers like they're a gift. **But they come with a lot of responsibility.**"

Miles hurried out into the city to start fighting crime. Soon, a TV news crew noticed him. They asked him for an interview.

"I'm just trying to do my neighborhood on Fourteenth Street proud," Miles said.

Peter watched the news, shocked. What was Miles thinking? Elsewhere, Smythe and Osborn were watching, too. Now everyone knew where the missing spider DNA was!

DBC · A NEW SPIDER-MAN?

PPREHENDS PURSE THIEF · MAYOR CONTINUES CAMPAIGN, SHOWS NO SIGNS OF SLOWING · FIRE ON WASHIN

Miles found the bullies who had pushed him around. With his new powers, it was easy to scare them.

Then Spider-Man swung down. Miles was so excited to meet him! But Spidey had a warning for Miles: **"Be careful not to become a bully yourself."**

"This is my neighborhood," Miles shot back, "and I want to make sure everyone feels safe."

"That's another thing," Spider-Man said as they swung to a nearby roof. "You shouldn't be giving away so much personal information."

"Please," said Miles. "No one's coming after me."

CRASH!

A giant purple robot stomped into view.

"New spider!" came Spencer Smythe's voice. "I have come for you!"

Spider-Man told Miles to run, but Miles was excited to team up with his hero. "We'll smash him!" Miles said. "There's two of us and only one of him!"

KEE-CRACK!

Another huge robot landed on the street behind them. But this one was being controlled by Alistair Smythe. It was the Spider-Men versus father and son!

Miles and Spider-Man jumped into battle. Then Miles felt a strange buzzing.

"Ahh!" he yelled. "What's happening in my head?"

Spider-Man grabbed Miles, just before the purple robot shot a net of green energy at him.

"It's called your spider-sense," Spidey explained. "And it means you need to move!"

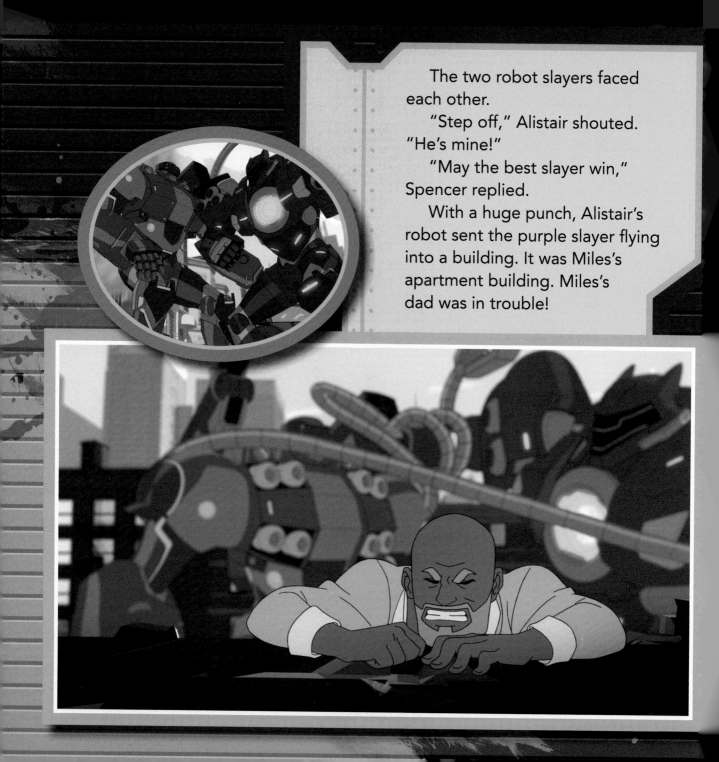

The two robot slayers faced each other.

"Step off," Alistair shouted. "He's mine!"

"May the best slayer win," Spencer replied.

With a huge punch, Alistair's robot sent the purple slayer flying into a building. It was Miles's apartment building. Miles's dad was in trouble!

Miles swung down just in time and saved his father!
But the purple robot reached down and picked
Miles up in its giant fist. Spider-Man shot his webs. He
was trying to save Miles.
"Spider-Man was right," Miles grunted.
"Never should have told them where I live."

Alistair didn't want Spencer to win. A machine in the maroon slayer's chest started to swirl into a giant vacuum. Miles's dad and Spider-Man were being pulled toward the maroon robot. Miles couldn't break free of the purple robot's grip. He started to panic.

"Leave them *alone*!" he cried. Then he felt a charge building in his body. A wave of red lightning shot out of Miles and blasted the slayers!

Spider-Man was surprised. "Whoa, he can do that?!"

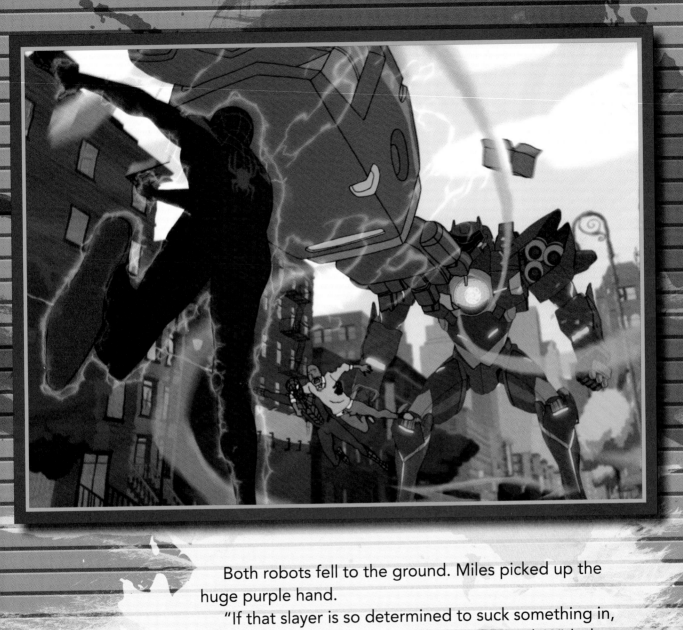

Both robots fell to the ground. Miles picked up the huge purple hand.

"If that slayer is so determined to suck something in, **let's give him what he wants!**" Miles said. With that, Miles sent the electro-burst surging into the robot hand and threw it as hard as he could.

Then, while it was still crackling with lightning, Miles heaved the hand at the maroon slayer's chest. It flew right into the vacuum, **and the maroon robot shorted out!**

Spencer Smythe hit a button and ejected from his slayer. He soared through the air, heading down toward the street.

Spencer landed in a nearby alley, where the two bullies were hanging out. "Out of my way, worms," he snarled, "or I'll wipe the street with you."

Then Miles landed right in front of him. "*Nobody* bullies the people in my neighborhood."

While Spidey tied Spencer up with webs, the bullies cheered for their friendly neighborhood Spider-Man.

Back at the apartment building, Miles's father approached the two heroes. "Excuse me," he said, "I just wanted to thank you."

"Oh, uh, anytime," Miles replied. His dad didn't know who he was! Miles realized that doing the right thing—the *powerful* thing—meant keeping his identity secret.

But he could still fight crime as **the newest, the ultimate . . .** *Spider-Man!*